Puppy, Puppy, Puppy

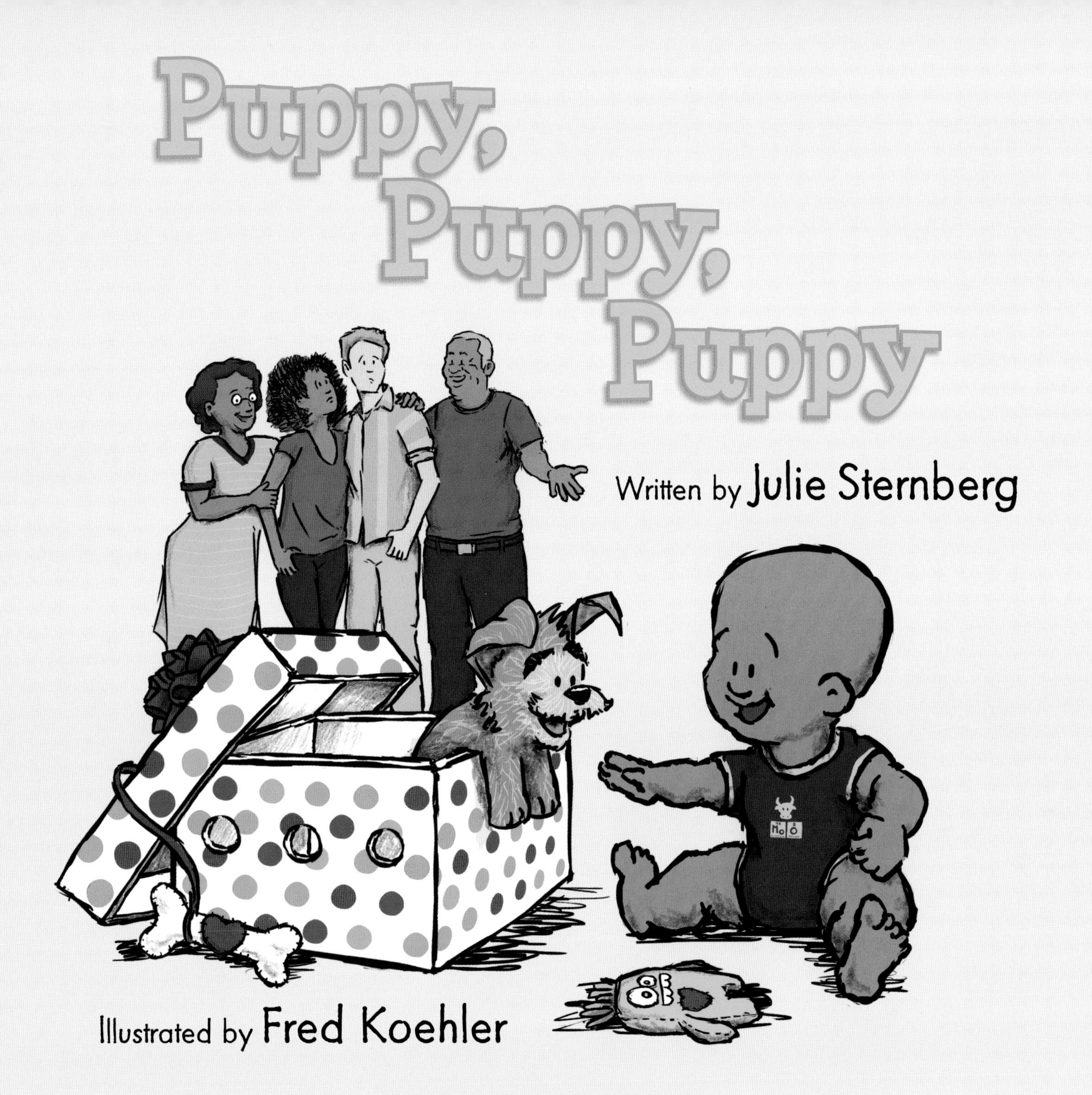

Written by Julie Sternberg

Illustrated by Fred Koehler

BOYDS MILLS PRESS
AN IMPRINT OF HIGHLIGHTS
Honesdale, Pennsylvania

Boyds Mills Press
An Imprint of Highlights
815 Church Street
Honesdale, Pennsylvania 18431

Printed in China
ISBN: 978-1-62979-466-2
Library of Congress Control Number: 2016942361

First edition
The text of this book is set in Futuramano Light.
The illustrations are done digitally.

10 9 8 7 6 5 4 3 2

For Bibi
—*JS*

For Big Shawn & Carole, Little Shawn, Vivian & Toby
—*FK*

As the sun rises,
Baby enjoys breakfast,
and Puppy enjoys breakfast.
And Baby says,
"Puppy."

Baby gets dressed nicely,
and Puppy gets dressed nicely.
And Baby says,

"Puppy."

Baby works in the garden,
and Puppy works in the garden.
And Baby says,

"Puppy."

Baby bathes in one tub,
and Puppy bathes in another.

But not for long.

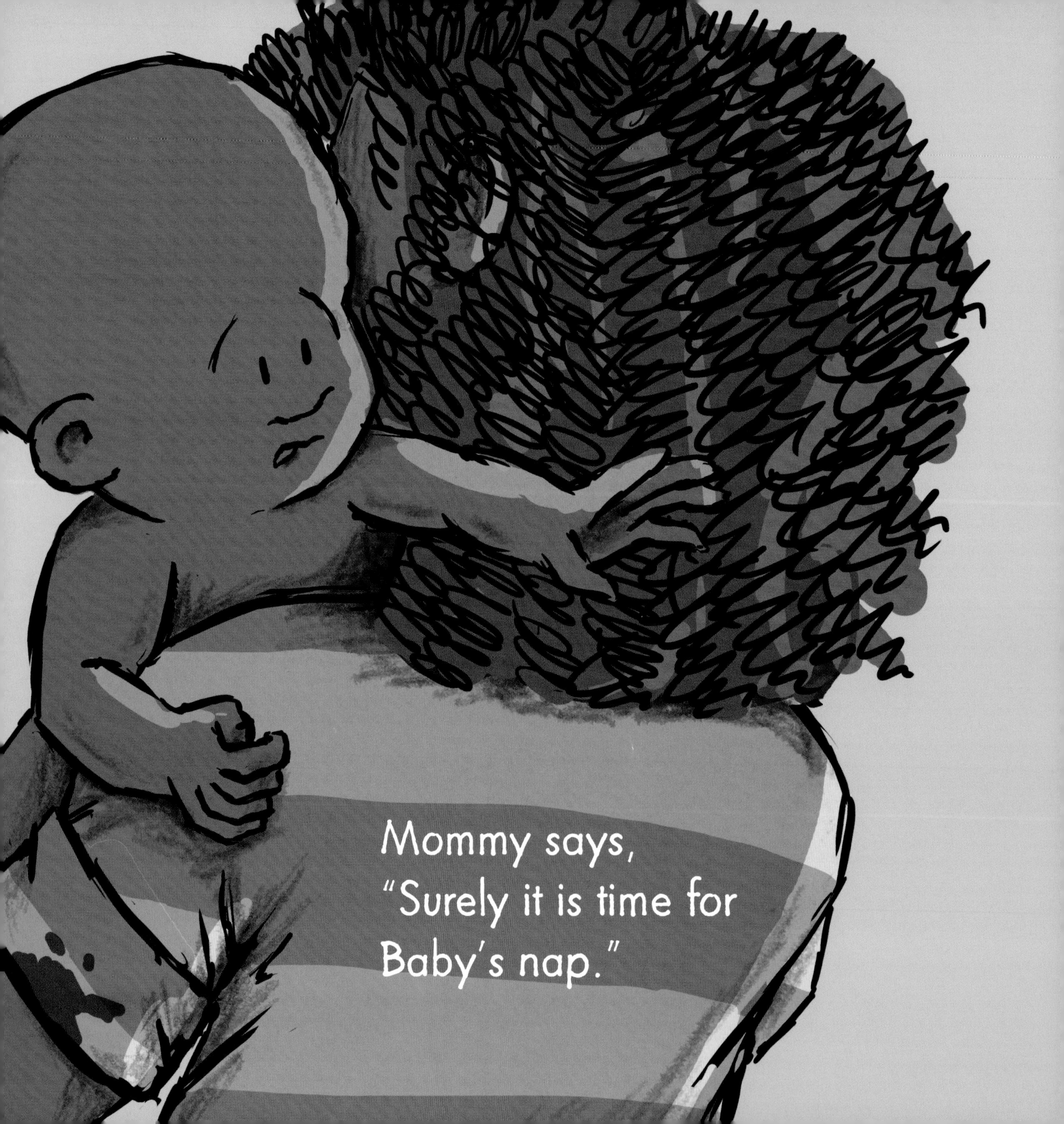
Mommy says,
“Surely it is time for
Baby’s nap.”

"Yes," Daddy says.
"It is surely time for
Baby's nap."

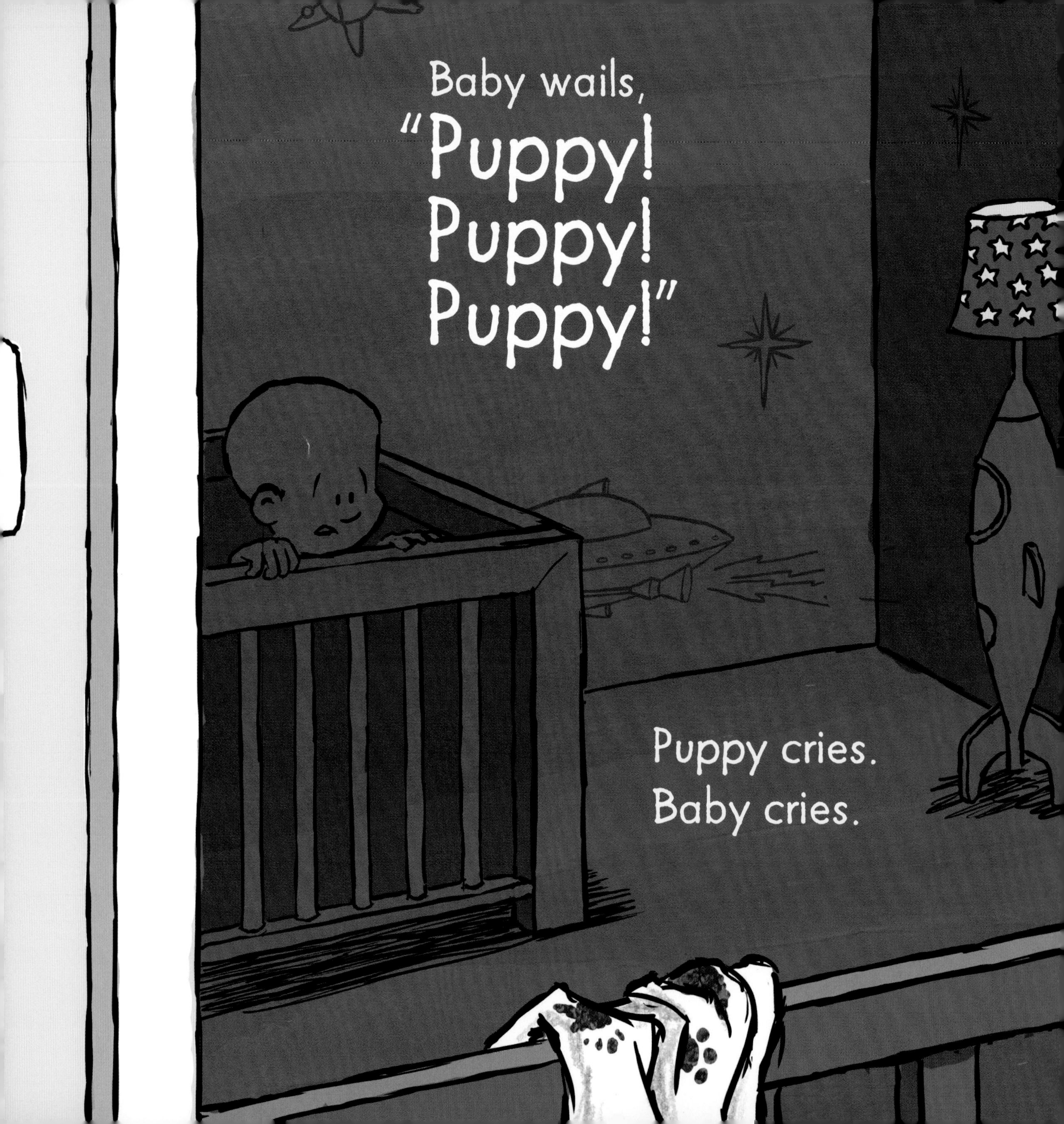

Baby wails,
"Puppy!
Puppy!
Puppy!"

Puppy cries.
Baby cries.

Mommy and Daddy say,
"Shh, Puppy. Puppy, shh.
Shh, shh, shh."

"Puppy?
Puppy?"

"PUPPY!"

Baby stays beside Puppy.

Puppy stays beside Baby.

Every single second.

No matter what.

And when the sun sets,
Baby and Puppy get
ready for bed together.

They howl at the moon together.

They sleep through
the night together.

Until dawn breaks
and Baby wakes.

And Baby says,

"Puppy, Puppy,
Puppy."